The Mercenary Lover

The Mercenary Lover

Eliza Haywood

MINT EDITIONS

The Mercenary Lover was first published in 1728.

This edition published by Mint Editions 2021.

ISBN 9781513291550 | E-ISBN 9781513294407

Published by Mint Editions®

 MINT
EDITIONS

minteditionbooks.com

Publishing Director: Jennifer Newens
Design & Production: Rachel Lopez Metzger
Project Manager: Micaela Clark
Typesetting: Westchester Publishing Services

The Preface

*S*o many Stories, meerly the Effect of a good Invention, having been publish'd as real Facts, I think it proper to inform my Reader, that the following Pages are fill'd with a sad, but true Account of the Misfortunes of a Family, living in the Metropolis of one of the finest Islands in the World; and happen'd in the Neighbourhood of a celebrated Church, in the Sound of whose Bells the Inhabitants of that populous City think it an Honour to be born.

The Character of the Mercenary Lover, *black and detectable as it is, wou'd yet have been more shocking, had I inserted some Passages of his former Life; but tho' the Baseness and Cruelty of his Disposition was not less conspicuous in someother of his Actions than in this last, of which I have made mention, yet the Persons ruin'd by him being of inferior Merit, I chose rather to confine myself to that, where neither the Tyes of Affinity, nor the Charms of Beauty, Innocence and Virtue, cou'd be a sufficient Protection from his destructive Artifices, than to run on with a long Detail of particular Vices which all seem complicated in this one.*

How little are the ill judging Multitude capable of chusing for themselves! How far are Wealth and Beauty, the two great Idols of the admiring World, from being real Blessings to the Possessors of them! With what numberless Dangers are their Attractions accompanied! and into what fatal Inadvertancies do they frequently plunge those who place their Dependance on them.

In a little Town, more famous for the wholesomeness of its Air, than Magnificence of its Buildings, or any other remarkable Qualification, there liv'd two Sisters, Co-heiressess of a very plentiful Estate; the younger of them, whose Name was *Miranda*, being of an airy, gay Disposition, gave Way to the Addresses of as many as had any Pretentious to merit a favourable Reception: But *Althea* the Elder being naturally more reserv'd and grave, was extreamly cautious who the entertain'd; and as she seem'd little ambitious of creating Admiration, was also not very inclinable to pay it: Hope, being the chief Food of Love, (especially in an Age where few Men, like the Heros of Antiquity, can patiently submit to a seven Years Service, before they receiv'd the Reward of a Kiss of the Hand the afforded so little of that, that she had but few of those who declar'd themselves her Lovers, in Comparison with the Number who watch'd the Smiles of the eternally gay *Miranda*.

Among those who endeavour'd at the Secret to please this celebrated Toast, none had more Reason to flatter himself with Hopes of Success than young *Clitander*, an Inhabitant of the Metropolitan City of this Island; and tho' of no higher Rank than a Trader, had a Paternal Estate, which, together with his great Business, made his Fortune on an Equivolent with that of *Miranda*: To add to this he had a very agreeable Person, and was Master of Accomplishments rare to be found in a Man of his Station: In fine, he was such as *Miranda* liked, and of the Multitude who address'd her, he alone had the Power of inspiring her with a real Passion, all others who pretended to her serv'd but to amuse her Vanity, the trifling Divertors of her gayer Moments; but *Clitander* in a small Time became the solid Business of her most serious Inclinations; when present, she felt a Pain-mix'd-Pleasure; and when absent, an Uneasiness, a certain Restlessness of Mind, which is the infallible Demonstrative of Love. He was too well acquainted with the Symptoms of that Passion not to perceive he had inspir'd her with a Share of it, sufficient to encourage him to expect everything from it which he could desire; and redoubling his Attacks, prest her in a Manner so undeniable, that he not only obtain'd from her a Promise of Marriage, but also saw, that as one Step towards the Performance of it, she banish'd all others who made Professions of the same Nature his was, from her House. It would be needless to detain my Reader with an immaterial Repetition of the Acknowledgments he made for this Condescension, the Behaviour of a Lover in the like happy Circumstance, is too generally known to want an Information; and if the Sequel of this Story should prove him not in Reality possest of the Passion he pretended, yet it will infer that he had Aims which were fully answer'd by the favourable Sentiments they had of him. I shall therefore pass over in Silence those Particulars, which without my Assistance may easily be guess'd at, and only say, That everything being agreed, and the Relations on both Sides perfectly satisfy'd as to Matters of Joynture and Settlements, these seemingly happy Pair were in a short Time united by a Tye, which ought to be indissolvable but by Death. They were married, and *Miranda* grew so perfectly fond of her agreeable Citizen, that in Conformity to the Notions and Behaviour of those she came to live among, she entirely threw off the gay Coquet, and began to dress, look, speak, and act in everything as became a Person of the Station she had taken on her. *Clitander* on the other Hand express'd the utmost Pleasure at this Alteration of her Conduct, appear'd the most indulging Husband, as she did the most obliging Wife, and they were look'd on by all who knew them, as the most exemplary Patterns of Conjugal Affection.

'Tis certain, indeed, that on one Side the Felicity was sincere and Compleat, *Miranda* truly lov'd, and believ'd herself as well belov'd; but alas! where is the Skill to trace, or Rules to reach the unfathomable Heart of artful Man, practis'd in Wiles, experienc'd in Deceit, amidst the many Turnings Search is lost; and the short Sight of Femal Penetration strives but in vain to pierce the hidden Depth: If a long Series of continu'd Courtship, if Longings, Ardours, and Impatiencies before Possession, cou'd denote a true and perfect Passion, if the most eager Transports, oft repeated Vows, and tender Pressures afterwards, might evince the Person faithful, *Clitander* had been the most enamour'd and most constant Man on Earth, and *Miranda* been as blest in *Reality*, as she was now in *Imagination*. But his was not a Soul capable of being touch'd with the Charms either of the Body or the Mind; Beauty, Virtue, or good Humour, he look'd on as Things indifferent, and not at all essential to the Happiness of Life,—Money was the only Darling of his mercenary Wishes, and as the Estate of which *Miranda* was Coheiress, was the sole Inducement to his addressing and marrying her; so by that Means being possest by that Moiety of it which was her Proportion, he now began to grow anxious for the other also, and put Invention on a continual Rack for some Contrivance to bring the long'd for Aim about.

The serious and reserv'd Temper of *Althea* gave him Hopes that she would not very easily be brought to listen to any Proposals; but as a verse as she had hitherto declar'd herself, he knew not how soon the Minute might arrive which might make an Alteration in her Sentiments in Favour of some Youth, who she might think worthy to create that Change: Love, he knew, was a Passion which comes swift and sudden on the Heart; his Business therefore was, to prevent as much as possible all Overtures of that Kind being made to her. To that End, under the Pretence of Affection to his Wife, he scarce ever suffer'd her to be from their House, and by a thousand Artifices, of which he was a perfect Master, so wound himself into her Esteem, that the thought there was not so excellent a Man on Earth: All he said she listened to as miraculous Truth, admir'd all he did, as the Effects of the strictest Honour, and most tender Friendship.

Having gain'd this Influence over her, there was little need to fear she would take any Affair in Hand, much less one of so great Consequence as Marriage was, without consulting him, and that it was now absolutely in his power to dissuade her from entertaining any Man, however agreeable in Person or in Fortune, who should make his Addresses to her on that Score; yet, notwithstanding he knew all this, nay had heard her frequently declare, That to the Aversion she ever had for Marriage, she had now another Motive added, to induce her to continue in a single Life, which was, that she wou'd rather that Part of the Estate she was possest of shou'd at her Death descend to him and his Heirs, than any other Person in the World, all was not sufficient to content him,—there was a possibility that these fine Promises might one Day be broke,—*Althea* was beautiful as an Angel and very young, tho' one Year older than his Wife,—he knew there were a thousand dying for her, and cou'd not be easy when he reflected that there was anything in the Power of Fate which cou'd put a Bar to his avaritious Views, which in a little Time he became so resolutely bent to compass, that he had recourse to Stratagems, the most inhumane and base, that ever enter'd into the Heart of Man. He was sometimes tempted to marry her to some indigent Wretch, who for a trifling Sum wou'd be glad to make over to him before-hand the Acres he should be Master of when made her Husband; at others, the *Demous*, whole Assistance he invok'd, suggested to him to get her trappan'd on board a Ship, and transported to some uninhabitable Shore, where she shou'd be left to perish on the Rocks, or be devour'd by the wild Denizons of the Woods and Mountains, but both these Designs were rejected, almost as soon as formed, not that to any relenting Thoughts they ow'd their Banishment, but there was Danger in them; he dreaded the Discovery of the Villany he wish'd to practise, and for that Reason cou'd not resolve to take any Measures wherein a second Person must be consulted, who perhaps, might sometime or other, either through Remorse or Malice, betray the whole Affair, and expose him to the Censure and Punishment his Crime deserv'd. The base are always Cowards, the same Meaness of Spirit which makes them the one, inclines them to the other also; they are ever in Fear, and while there remains even the smallest Probability of Danger, Peace is a Stranger to their Minds. *Clitander* therefore resolv'd to trust no other but himself, in the Execution of whatever Project he shou'd put in Practise, and the Difficulty there was to find one, in which there was not an absolute Necessity for a Confederate, kept him for some Months in a Perplexity not to be conceiv'd.

Yet so admirably was he vers'd in the Art of Dissimulation, that tho' his Soul was full of the most poynant Anxiety, his Countenance was all serene and calm as an unruffled Sky; upon his oilly Tongue the most melting Accents in soft Persuasion hung, and Tenderness unspeakable languish'd in his Eyes; gay Smiles play'd round his Mouth in dimpl'd Graces, and his whole Air was Harmony and Love: None but the All-feeing Eye of Heaven cou'd penetrate into his Heart, or guess at the Perfidiousness that harbour'd there. Never did two Persons think themselves more happy than did *Miranda* and her amiable Sister, the one in being possest of the best of Men and Husbands, and the other in a most sincere Friend and disinterested Relation. A perfect Amity and uninterrupted Chearfulness, seem'd to reign throughout this little Family—They were the Envy of their Neighbours, the Delight of their Acquaintance, and the Pride of their Servants:—So much is the World, and even our selves deceiv'd by Appearances, and how little are we capable of distinguishing the real Felicity from the Shadow of one? Those who believed themselves, and were by all believ'd to be in a State of the most fixed Tranquility that could be, were in Effect on the Brink, and ready to plunge into a Gulph of Destruction, as much to be trembled at, as their imaginary Comfort was before to be desir'd and covered.

The working Brain of the industriously mischievous *Clitander*, at last furnished him with a Design, in the Success of which he promis'd himself a double Pleasure: Tho' Avarice was his prevailing Vice, and the Love of Money had so entire a Possession of his Soul, that no other Charms had Power to inspire him with a real Passion, yet was he not without those Desires which are too frequently mistaken for the Influence of the god of tender Sighs: The Beauties of *Althea*, and the Freedoms he enjoy'd with her as a Brother, had sometimes given him Emotions, such as Lovers feel, tho' unaccompanied with that Respect and Tenderness which those who are truly worthy of that Name must pay to the ador'd Object,—With strong and vehement Desires he burn'd to enjoy her, and when in *Miranda's* Arms, languished to rifle the untasted Loveliness of her beauteous Sister.—He plotted therefore, how first to fatiate this Passion, which, once obtain'd, he thought would be the most effectual Means to gratify the other also; and determin'd to make her guilty before he made her wretched: He soon began to put in Execution this most detestable Invention, by all those Artifices of which he was a perfect Master, and for which, indeed, he seem'd design'd by Nature, who had given him a Countenance and Manner of Behaviour so vastly distant from his sordid Disposition.

To corrupt a young Maid of *Althea's* reserv'd Humour, bred up in the strictest Principles of Virtue, and unacquainted even with an unchast Thought, would have seem'd a Task too difficult to be accomplish'd, and with Reason have deterr'd any other Man from an Attempt that Way: But *Clitander*, as he was not only possest of more bodily Perfections than the generality of his, so he had also been more successful with the Fair; seldom had he been repuls'd, but often a Conqueror over the most seemingly obdurate Hearts.—He knew the Influence he had gain'd over that of *Althea*, and tho' it was only contracted under the Notion of Friendship, that That Passion was a very good Preparative for the other which he aim'd to inspire.—The Name of Husband to her Sister, was at first some little Impediment to his Hopes, but then the Consideration how many Opportunities that Title gave him, which were deny'd to all other Men, satisfy'd his Doubts, and made him not fear but that a little Time and Assiduity, might by Degrees steal into her Soul those Inclinations which wou'd give him the absolute Possession of his Wishes.

The first Step he made towards the Accomplishment of this barbarous Enterprize, was to redouble the Civilities and Tendernesses with which he had been accustom'd to treat *Althea*, and knowing she was naturally a great Lover of Reading, took Care to bring her home everyday something new for her Amusement; I say Amusement, for I believe the Reader will easily imagine, the Books he desir'd she should peruse, were neither Religion, Philosophy, nor Morality; there are certain gay Treatises which insensibly melt down the Soul, and make it fit for amorous Impressions, such as the Works of *Ovid*, the late celebrated *Rochester*, and many other of more modern Date, and of this Kind it was that he furnish'd the Study of his intended Victim, to the two worst Passions of deprav'd Humanity.

The Affairs of her Family often calling *Miranda* away, gave him, who now scarce ever stirr'd from home, many Opportunities of entertaining her alone: All which he imploy'd to the best Advantage for his Designs; not that he ever in the least declar'd himself a Lover, but artfully, and as tho' it were by Accident, introduc'd a Discourse on the Force of Love, always undertaking to prove, That whatever were the Consequences of that Passion they ought not to be condemn'd, because they were unavoidable,—Nay, sometimes went so prophanely far, as to make Holy Writ the Dupe to his Designs, bringing Instances from that to argue, that Incest was no Crime. Had the modest Soul of *Althea* been in the least appriz'd of the Aim of these Conversations, so different from what she had ever been accustom'd to hear, the Shock of such a Discovery had at once stop'd her Ears from listening to Doctrine so pernicious, but as she was far from suspecting anything of his Inclinations, and took an infinite Pleasure in hearing him talk, by little and little the Poison of his Infectious Precepts gain'd Ground on her Belief; and finding herself wholly incapable of defending the Cause of Virtue against those Arguments which his superior Wit and Genius brought, began to think, indeed, that what he said was just, and that those Laws which prohibited a free Commerce between the Sexes, were only the Boundaries of Policy, invented to keep Mankind in Awe, and restrain the Sallies of Nature, which otherwise wou'd involve the World in a general Confusion.

Soon did he perceive the Ground he had gain'd, and exulted at the Success of his Insinuations: Not doubting now, but that he should be able to persuade her to anything, he began to appear more open, wou'd often take her Hand and kiss it with Raptures, such as, had she accustom'd herself to receive Addresses of that Nature, she wou'd have presently known to have been the Effects of that Passion which is commonly call'd Love.—When ever he look'd upon her, his well instructed Eyes seem'd to shoot Glances of an unuterable Tenderness,— whenever he spoke to her, it was in the fondest, most endearing Terms that Love and Wit cou'd form.—Yet so innocent, so unexperienc'd was she in the destructive Passion and the betraying Wiles of Man, that all these Symptoms were not sufficient to alarm, nor warn her of the Danger. Unknowing, therefore, what was doing in her own Soul, she gave Way to all the Liberties he took, and became all disolv'd, lost in a Tide of Love before she imagin'd herself threaten'd by even its most distant Approaches.

But it was not so with him, he read the State of her Mind in the soft Languishments of her shining Eyes, and in her balmy Sighs, when presuming on the Authority of a Brother, he sometimes took her in his Arms, felt the Alteration he had made, and was too well convinc'd that his Work was compleated; and he had nothing now to do, but to declare himself, and boldly seize his Wishes.

Since the fatal Discovery of her Sentiments some Days elaps'd, without giving him any Opportunity for the Accomplishment of his Designs; but at length Fortune, hitherto too much a Friend to this Traitor to all Honour and Fidelity, afforded him one as ample as he cou'd have wish'd. *Miranda* went to make a Visit to a Relation who liv'd at the Town where both she and *Althea* had receiv'd their Birth and Education; she wou'd have persuaded her Sister to accompany her, but the ill Stars of that unfortunate Lady, wou'd not suffer her to comply with her Desires; and the other perceiving her refractory, wou'd not press her beyond her Inclination. The Distance between that Place to which she was gone, and the great City in which they liv'd being about three Miles, her perfidious Husband was secure that the wou'd not return till Night. And scarce ever had his Eyes beheld a Sight so joyful as the Departure of the Coach which bore away that Impediment to his Hopes, his Wife.

She was no sooner gone, than he ran up to the Chamber of *Althea*, where she happen'd to be fitting indulging her innocent Meditations, and altogether unsuspicious of approaching Ruin: After some previous Discourse on ordinary Subjects, he began to talk of Marriage and the Unhappiness of that State, when both the Parties so join'd were not content with their Lot.—How much, my lovely Sifter, shou'd I lament, said he, shou'd I ever see you one of those complaining Wives, your Wit despis'd, your good Humour subservient to a lordly and imperious Husband's Rule, your Beauty, all that inestimable Stock of Charms with which you are so divinely stor'd, unprais'd, unlov'd, and perhaps scorn'd even to your Face,—such a Behaviour is too frequent, and shou'd it be your Fate, O most adorable *Althea*, continu'd he, with a Voice which seem'd interrupted by his Sighs, how very wretched, how accurst wou'd be *Clitander* to know and want the Power to ease your Mournings or revenge your Wrongs! Wou'd to Heaven, answer'd the unsuspecting Maid, I cou'd as easily return the Obligations I have to your generous Care, as I can secure myself from all Apprehensions of those Miseries you so well describe,—the Merits of *Clitander* have freed me from the Danger of becoming an abandon'd Wife,—two such Husbands are not to be the Portion of one Family,—I despair to find a Man like him, and cannot submit to accept a Happiness inferior to that my Sister enjoys.

Tho' these Words were spoken with the most perfect Innocence, they were notwithstanding the Overflowings of a Soul wholly devoted to him, and sincerely taken up with Tenderness, and Admiration of his imaginary Virtues: And well discerning from what Source they sprung, Thou Angel of thy Sex, said he, taking her in his Arms, how happy shou'd I think myself, cou'd I believe it was, indeed, your good Opinion of me, which defended you from list'ning to the Insinuations of the less faithful Part of Mankind,—but alas! pursu'd he, intently fixing his Eyes on hers, as tho' he wou'd look into her Soul, I dare not flatter my fond Desires so far, and had I in *Miranda*'s Stead address'd *Althea*, shou'd have been among the Number of those her Scorn has render'd miserable. I must not then have known your Worth, resum'd she, and if you think *Althea* as capable of judging what is truly valuable, as you have found *Miranda*, you must believe your Fate had been the same with one, as with the other Sister. Had it been so, cry'd he, in a well acted Transport, sure some kind Spirit wou'd have warn'd me of the Blessing,—some Dream wou'd have convey'd to me the Knowledge of your Goodness, and instructed by my Guardian Angel what to do, I had not thus err'd in my mistaken Choice. These Expressions utter'd with the utmost Warmth, and accompany'd by an Embrace more strenuous than before this Moment he had ever ventur'd to clasp her with, gave her a little Surprize, and starting from his Arms, and looking on him with a kind of Confusion in her Eyes, Do you not love *Miranda* then? said she. Dear as my Life, reply'd he, who wanted not Presence of Mind to extricate himself out of the most puzzling Difficulties, Never Man lov'd with a fonder, or more lasting Ardour than I my Wife,—but yet, continu'd he, with a Sigh, as if his Heart were bursting, while my Heart avows the Merits of *Miranda*, it cannot be unjust to the infinitely superior ones *Althea* boasts:—Should *Miranda* forgetful of her Marriage Vows, and ungrateful to the Tenderness I bear her, relinquish me, and seek new Joys in any others Arms, my abused Affection and my wounded Honour wou'd give me Pains intollerable, but shou'd *Althea*,—O the thought is Hell,—shou'd the adorable *Althea*, tho' bound by no Obligements, admit to her Embraces some Youth, more happy than *Clitander*, how much beyond the Reach of Words wou'd be the Horror of my distracted State!—I cou'd not hear it, but should commit some wild Extravagance might plunge us all in Ruin.—O *Althea*, pursu'd he, taking Advantage of the Astonishment he saw her in, and which prevented her from interrupting him, too lovely Maid pity your wretched Brother,—your Lover,—your Adorer;—the cold Returns of Friendship are Cordials too, too faint to keep the almost expiring Lamp of Life awake—O give me more, or withdraw them too, and kill me with your hate. He had no sooner pronounc'd these Words than he threw himself upon her Bosom, where, if the present Emotions of his Desires did not convulse him with real Agonies, he counterfeited them so well, that a Woman more experienc'd in those Racks of struggling Impatiencies than was *Althea*, might easily have mistaken them for Natural. But with what Words is it possible to represent the mingled Passions of *Althea*'s Soul, now perfectly instructed in his Meaning; Fear, Shame, and Wonder combating with the softer Inclinations, made such a wild Confusion in her Mind, that as the was about to utter the Dictates of the one, the other rose with contradicting Force, and stop'd the Accents e're she cou'd form them into Speech; in broken Sentences the sometimes seem'd to favour, then to discourage his Attempts, but all dissolv'd and melted down by that superior Passion, of which herself till now was ignoraut she had entertain'd, never had Courage to repel the growing Boldness, with which he every Moment encroach'd upon her Modesty, and when the most strove to say something which might dash his Hopes, cou'd bring forth no harsher Sounds than, Forbear, forbear my dangerous, and too lovely Brother! cruel *Clitander*, wou'd you ruin me? 'Tis easy to guess what the Consequences of such Sort of Repulses must be, and whether such a Behaviour wou'd not have been far from dissipating the Ardour of a Lover, less fiercely animated than was *Clitander*. He made but short Replies to her Entreaties or Interrogatories, speaking to her only in this Manner, O permit me to secure the Blessing you have so often promis'd,—let me assure myself you never will be another's,—be mine, and ease me of these Doubts Uncertainty creates.—Nor, indeed, wou'd it have been conformable to the rest of his Artifice to have held a long Conversation, or given her Time for Thought or Recollection, *Action* was now his Business, and in this Hurry of her Spirits, all unprepar'd, incapable of Defence, half yielding, half reluctant, and scarce sensible of what she suffer'd, he bore her trembling to the Bed, and perpetrated the cruel Purpose he had long since contriv'd.

The Scene of Ruin over, the barbarous Author of it, now began to exert his utmost Wit and Eloquence to dry her Tears, and hush the Remonstrances of violated Virtue; he enforc'd the Arguments she had before too fatally given Ear to, That the Ties of Blood or Affinity were but imaginary Bars to Love, pleaded the Violence of his Passion, and the absolute Necessity it brought, either to enjoy his wish or dye; swore ten thousand Oaths of an unalterable Constancy, and that the Secret never should be divulg'd.—The natural Propensity which all People have to listen to any Arguments which may serve to excuse the Errors they commit, join'd to the Corruption which his Insinuations had brought on her Principles, made her not aim at confuting anything he urg'd, either in his, or her own Vindication; and of all the Passions which had so lately ruffled her Soul, Love and Shame were only now remaining: By repeated and endearing Familiarities he endeavour'd to strengthen the one, and entirely dissipate the other; but the Confusion of her Mind was so great, that tho' he stirr'd not from her the whole Day, he found all his Efforts to compose her ineffectual; and at her Sisters Return, the Sight of that wrong'd Lady overwhelm'd her with a Disorder which had been sufficient to have made some Women suspicious of the Truth. The villainous Occasion of it, apprehensive of the Danger, and also to prevent any Notice being taken of his having been all Day in the Chamber of *Althea*, if the Servants shou'd happen to speak of it, with an unparallel'd Assurance, taking his Wife in his Arms as soon as ever the enter'd the Room, I am glad you are come home my Dear, said he, *Althea* is quite spoil'd with the Vapours, and tho' I have been complaisant enough not to leave her a Moment since you went out, all I can do to bring her into good Humour is but Labour thrown away;—she will, in spite of me, indulge her Chagrin, and will give no other Reason for it, than that she had an ugly Dream last Night. *Miranda* laugh'd at this idle Superstition (as she call'd it) in her Sister, and began to rally her on the ill Effects of a too thoughtful Disposition; till the other (who long'd to be alone, to give a Loose to Reflection) answer'd her in so peevish a Maner, that she seem'd in good Earnest affected with that Distemper *Clitander* had accus'd her of; and what was really the Effects of Remorse might very well be taken for ill Humour. *Miranda* continued her pleasantry for sometime, but finding it of no Effect on her Sister, Come my Dear, said she, taking her Husband by the Hand, let us leave her to herself,—if we stay here much longer, we too shall catch the Contagion.—As she spoke these Words they both quitted the Room. *Clitander* as he was going out, turning back to make her a submissive Bow, accompany'd with the most tender and endearing Air that Love cou'd teach him to assume.

Althea now left to the Freedom of her Thoughts, felt a kind of Pleasure, in giving Way to Pain; and in not checking the Struggles of departing Virtue, found the Means to ease herself of its Remorse,— She accus'd her easy Nature, wonder'd how she cou'd be so lost, so abandon'd by all the Principles her Youth was taught, and curst the Tenderness which had betray'd her,—the Wrong she had done her Sister, the Dishonour she had brought on herself, the Crime she had been guilty of to Heaven, all appear'd to her distracted Imagination in their blackest and most damning Colours, and for some Moments involv'd her in so terrible a Dispair, that she was almost ready to lay desperate Hands on her own Life, thereby to put a Period to the Shame of it. But as Things violent are seldom of any long Continuance, the Force of these Emotions in a few Moments were evaporated and spent; and the Idea of *Clitander*, his Charms, his Fondness, and imagin'd Honour and Sweetness of Disposition, took their Turn to triumph over the faint Remains of Modesty and Virtue; and the Felicity of being belov'd by a Man, whom she consider'd as the Wonder of his Sex, seem'd to her sufficient Reparation for that she had resign'd in the rewarding it; and the Gratitude she ow'd his Passion, an Excuse for the Crime her own had influenc'd her to commit. In fine, the Morning found her as calm and compos'd as she had been the Night before the contrary; and if there was left in her Soul any Tincture of her former Disquiet, the Endearments of *Clitander*, and the Arguments he made use of to reconcile her to what had past between them, entirely clear'd her of it, and made her willingly resign herself to frequent Repetitions of that guilty Joy, she had at first so much regretted.

In this Criminal Tranquility let us leave her for a while, and return to her Undoer: That cruel Brother, having thus satisfy'd the Cravings of his lawless Flame, and revell'd in the Spoils of violated Chastity, remain'd but a short Time contented with the Triumph he had gain'd, the Love of Money now resum'd its Empire in his sordid Soul; and as it was not so much the Possession of *Althea*'s Person as her Estate, which had induc'd him to take this Pains, so having obtain'd the one, he now began to set his whole Wits at Work to become Master of the other also. 'Tis true, he was not in that Anxiety of Mind he had been, because having the free Possession of *Althea*, he was pretty secure from any Apprehensions of her marrying, at least while he continu'd to treat her with that Tenderness which had so fatally seduc'd her; but being in all his Passions, except Avarice, extreamly inconstant, he soon grew satiated with the unrestrain'd Enjoyment, and consequently weary of dissembling Ardours he cou'd no longer feel.—In those very Moments, when most he swore he lov'd, he curst her in his Heart; and with his Vows of everlasting Fondness, mix'd Imprecations and Wishes for her Death,—had the Means of it, without Danger of Discovery, been in his Power, 'tis certain she had not long surviv'd her Loss of Honour; but to the same Fears which had before Enjoyment been her Protection, was she still indebted to for her Safety; and tho' he was always contriving her Destruction, he cou'd not, with all the Invention he was Master of, find the Way to bring it about.

In this Dilemma he receiv'd a considerable Addition to the Perplexity he was before involv'd in, which was the Knowledge that *Althea* was with Child; the Dread which seiz'd his guilty Soul, whenever he consider'd how Difficult it would be to keep the incestuous Secret from Discovery, fill'd him with Horrour almost proportion'd to his Crime,—but so great a Master was he of Presence of Mind, that not all the Confusion of his Thoughts prevented him from prosecuting his Designs: He no sooner knew the Condition *Althea* was in, but to add to the Melancholy of it, he was continually filling her Ears with Stories of Women who had died in Child-birth, wou'd sometimes, in a well counterfeited Terrour tell her, he had heard a Weasel squeak, at others, that a Raven had perch'd upon the House, pretend some ominous Dream: In fine, scarce a Day pass'd over without his bringing her an account of some fabulous Prediction, till he wrought so far on the Weakness of her Sex, as to settle her in the Belief that she should not out-live the Time prefix'd by Nature for her being deliver'd of her Burthen. Having gain'd this Point, as he was sitting alone with her one Day, taking her by the Hand, and dissembling the most perfect Tenderness, My most ador'd, my forever dear *Althea*, said he, I have a Proposal to offer to you, which I have long wish'd to speak, but never had the Courage, fearing it shou'd encrease that Melancholly to which already you are but too much inclin'd,—but my Angel, continued he, if you wou'd but make use of your good Sense to arm you against these womanish Apprehensions, you wou'd not think yourself nearer to Death for being prepar'd for it. Here he paus'd, expecting she wou'd desire an Explanation of these Words, which she immediately did, not a little surpriz'd what it was he meant by them. Since you command me, resum'd he, I will no longer delay to reveal what for sometime has created me many Inquietudes.—Shou'd you, pursu'd he, with a Sigh, which Heaven forbid, in giving Life to the dear Product of our Love, resign your own, the Estate you are possest of must, of Consequence, you dying without a *Will*, descend to your Sister, and the Children born of her become the Inheritors,—it will not be in my Power to prevent it, and that most precious Pledge of the most fond Affection that ever fill'd the Heart of Man, must be a Beggar, a poor Dependant on an unhappy Father, who can do no more than make some mean Provision for it, as for the Child of some Acquaintance or remote Relation, while those begotten on *Miranda*, tho' far less dear, favour'd by Legitimacy, shall riot in the Plenty of your Lands, and look with Scorn on the wrong'd Babe, whose Birthright makes them rich.—The Thought of this is worse than Death to me, and will be so to you, when once you come to know a Mother's Pangs, a Mother's Tenderness and Care;—I wou'd have you, therefore, to provide against it, and by a *Testament* legally drawn and sign'd by Witnesses, cut off *Miranda*, and secure your Child from all those Injuries which Want Occasions. How can that be? interrupted *Althea*, we know not of what Sex the wretched Infant is, and in a *Will*, the Name, as well as Relative must punctually be set down. For that I have laid a Scheme, reply'd he, rejoic'd to find her in so compliable a Disposition, you shall bequeath your Lands, your Money, Jewels, and whatsoever valuable Goods you have to a fictitious Person,—we may easily invent a Name;—and because it may be expected he should appear to claim the Benefit of the Will, I must be left *Trustee*, or if you please, his *Guardian*, and your *Executor*,—by this Means I shall have the Opportunity of doing Justice to my Child, since being myself, in Right of my Wife, next Heir, none has a Privilege to scrutinize into the Reasons of your having made so seemingly strange a *Will*; and thus will also, your Reputation, even after Death, remain unfully'd; and the worst the prying World can say, will be, that you were unnatural, and the Tenderness for that, which ought to be most dear, be taken for the Want of it, to your Sister. He said no more, nor indeed had he any Occasion for further Arguments, what he had already urg'd appear'd too reasonable for her to deny Assent: She very much approv'd, and thank'd his seeming Care, and the same Evening gave him Commission to go to a Lawyer, and have the *Will* drawn up according as he had advis'd.

Fortune, and the Credulity of the too fond *Althea* had hitherto crown'd all his Endeavours with Success, and he began now to think there was no Difficulty which his Genius, Resolution, and the Fertility of his Invention cou'd not surmount.—He was not however, of the Disposition of some People, who lull themselves too soon in an imaginary Security, and transported with what they have already obtain'd, sit down enjoying the Reflection, contented before their Work is done: With the same indefatigable Industry with which he commenc'd his Designs, did he proceed to the Accomplishment of them.—Early as the Day did he arise next Morning, and having given Directions to an able Attorney, what he would have done, in a small Time after, brought to *Althea* a Parchment, which he told her was the *Will*, but which was in Reality, a Deed of Gift to himself, of all the Estate she was at that Instant in Possession of. But because my Reader will doubtless be amaz'd for what Reason he went about to deceive her in this Manner, his Wife being the undoubted Heir, I must unravel the Bottom of his Aim, and set forth a Design so monstruous, as were there not too many whom the sad Catastrophe made acquainted with the Truth, wou'd scarce gain Belief in any Mind, less prone to Villany than that of *Clitander*. Fir'd, as I have already said, with the repeated Possession of the Beauties of *Althea*, and burning with a yet unextinguish'd Passion for the Enjoyment of her Wealth, and to these two Motives for wishing her in another World being added, that of the Danger her Condition involv'd him in, of the Discovery of the Crime he had committed in debauching her, all together made him resolve to murder her, and to do it in such a Manner, as might have the Appearance of being acted by herself,—the Laws of the Nation depriving the Successors of Persons so desperate, of inheriting any Part of their Goods, he contriv'd to secure himself by a Deed of Gift, drawn up, dated and sign'd before there was any Appearance of her laying Hands on her Life.

But here, Heaven was pleas'd to put a Stop to his Proceedings, and what he thought wou'd be the most certain Means to secure the Accomplishment of his Hopes, prov'd the Ruin of them.—He came to *Althea*, and in a great Hurry, as if he fear'd the coming in of some Person who might interrupt what he was about to say, show'd her the Parchment, and unfolding only that Part of it where she should set her Hand, desir'd her to sign. Chance, more than Suspicion, made her desire to read it first; but that Demand a little alarming him, as not expecting she would scruple anything he requir'd, he was that Moment at a Stand how to reply, but recovering himself as well as he was able, told her there was no Occasion for her Perusal, for it was drawn up exactly as they had agreed, and that to look it over, wou'd take up more Time than she was aware of, and that probably her Sister, or someother of the Family might come up and catch her in that Employment. There is no Haste then, said she, for my signing it,—I shall scarce dye before tomorrow, and if you give it me, I will put it into my Cabinet, and read it when I am certain of no Interruption. Now was he indeed confounded, not all his Cunning or Assurance cou'd enable him presently to resolve what to do, in an Exigence so dangerous to all the Measures he had form'd; to leave it with her was to proclaim himself the Villain he was in Reality, and to refuse, was to give her Room to guess there was something in it of a different Kind from what he had made her believe: Making a Virtue, therefore, of Necessity, after a Moment's Thought, You do not consider, resum'd he, of what ill Consequence it may be, to keep such a Thing by you,—it may be found,—some Accident may betray the Affair,—I wou'd have this Secret lodg'd beyond the Reach of Fate itself:—Remember, pursu'd he more eagerly, 'tis for your Child you do it,—shou'd you neglect a Thing of so much Consequence to its Welfare; the unborn Babe may live to curse its too remiss and unkind Parent.—Bur, added he, perceiving she look'd amaz'd to hear him talk in this Manner, if you imagine I have caus'd anything to be inserted there which you can scruple to approve, I will sit down and read it to you. There may be more Danger in that, said she, than can be reasonably apprehended from lying in my Cabinet,—but you shall have your Will. In speaking these Words she shut the Door, and prepar'd herself to listen to him. The grave and determin'd Air with which she spoke and mov'd, made him easily perceive she was not perfectly pleas'd with his Behaviour; his natural Boldness, however, enabling him to go on, he unfolded the Parchment, shadding as well as he cou'd, with his Hand the Top of it, on which was written, *The Deed of Gift*, and began not to read, but to speak such Words as were suitable to the Instrument for which she had given Orders, what he utter'd being altogether different from the real Contents. The Hesitation of his Accents, and the Confusion which he cou'd not keep from being visible in his Countenance, having created in her Suspicions, to which before her Heart was wholly a Stranger, with the utmost Watchfulness she observ'd his every Look and Motion, and taking Notice that he endeavour'd to conceal some Part of the Writing, and also glancing her Eyes over it, perceiving that his Tongue consulted his own Invention more than the Parchment, she was both convinc'd and shock'd at the Deceit with which he treated her; and nothing is more to be wonder'd at than, that she, so far from all Artifice herself, cou'd all at once have her Eyes unseal'd to behold such monstruous Baseness and Hypocrisy in the Man, whose imaginary Honour and Fidelity she had forfeited all that was dear to her to reward, did not make her that Moment break out into some wild Extravagance of Rage, which thou'd have made him know his Wiles were now betray'd, and his deceiving Schemes no more cou'd boast their accustom'd Success.—'Tis certain that her Soul was all Surprize, Refentment and Confusion, yet did she bridle the rising Passions, and tho' half suffocated, restrain'd the swelling Sighs, forbid her Tears to flow, or Tongue to vent the smallest Title of her Discovery or Indignation, till having done reading, he once more entreated her to sign. Yes, said she, I will sign, but it shall be in Flames, as you hereafter must, for all the Miseries,— the eternal Ruin, your cursed Insinuations have brought on the undone *Althea.* These Expressions were accompany'd with a Torrent of Tears and at the same Time snatching the Parchment from his Hand, she threw it into a great Fire, which, the Weather being very cold, was then burning in the Room, where it was immediately consum'd. The Amazement in which this Action invol'd the Soul of *Clitander*, is not to be express'd;—he saw he was detected, and had nothing to alledge in his Excuse or Vindication,—the projecting *Demons*, who had prompted him to this Villany, now refus'd him their Assistance,—his once ready Wit and Invention now forsook him,—all his Powers abandon'd him,— his Eyes and Tongue forgot their usual Artifice,—Fear, Shame and Horror sat on each unguarded Feature, and all the naked Criminal appear'd in View;—with down-cast Looks a while he stood silent, revolving in his Mind a thousand black and terrible Ideas: And she recovering herself a little from that Excess of Passion, which had before stop'd the Uterance of her Words, went on in her Upbraidings in this Manner, Ungenerous, mean Designer as thou art, said she, how little didst thou know the lavish Fondness of *Althea*'s Soul, or thy own Power?—had I been Mistress of all the Globe contains, and been made sensible *Clitander* wanted it, with Pleasure I shou'd have yielded the unvalu'd Treasure, and thought myself more rich in his Acceptance, than in any other Blessing that Heaven and Fortune cou'd endow me with,—to that Degree I lov'd you, Words cannot speak how much,—no Description,—nothing but my Infatuation can set forth the vast Extent of that transcendant Passion with which I was inspir'd;— but know, it was not to your lovely *Person* alone you were indebted for the Proofs I gave you of it,—I figur'd you out to my admiring Soul as the most perfect Pattern of Fidelity and Honour, and thought I never cou'd too much acknowledge the Beauty of your *Mind*,—O! how have I been deceiv'd, continu'd she, bursting a second Time into Tears, how cruelly has my unwarry Innocence suffer'd itself to be impos'd on;— thou Monster of Hipocrisy, how wretched haft thou made me! The struggling Passions of her Soul made her unable to utter more, but what her Tongue fail'd to express, her streaming Eyes and agonizing Tremblings abundantly made up for. *Clitander* with much ado forcing himself to look upon her, demanded of her, but with a Voice wholly unassur'd and broken, What it was she meant? An Interrogatory of this Kind, appear'd to her to have so much Impudence in it, that it seem'd wholly to dissipate her Grief, to make Way for a more stormy Passion: Rage had now the whole Possession of her Breast, and she answer'd him in Terms which fully convinc'd him, if before he had any Doubt of it, that she had discover'd the Artifice of the pretended *Will*, and also that it would be no easy Matter to bring her to Moderation: He attempted it however as much as his Disorders wou'd give him Leave; but the more he aim'd to excuse what he had done, the more she grew incens'd; alledging, that tho' he had the highest Reasons for designing *a Deed of Gift* instead of a *Will*, which yet the cou'd not allow, she never cou'd forgive his Intention of deceiving her.—She told him, that since she found him capable of Artifice in one Thing, she doubted not but he had been so in all; and that she no more cou'd give Credit to anything that came from him.—All he cou'd say was ineffectual to move her from this Resolution, and he was oblig'd to leave her, having several Times been bid by her to leave the Room, without being able to work her to any Return of Softness, or even to look on him with less Resentment than that which both her Eyes and Tongue declar'd at the Time of her throwing the Parchment into the Fire.

It wou'd be as needless as impossible, to set forth, as it deserves, the distracted State in which this Night was past, both by *Clitander* and *Althea*, to be told what has happen'd between them, will better enable the Reader's Imagination to conceive their present Wretchedness than anything I am able to say.—The Deceiver and Deceiv'd felt equal Pains, the one in the Disappointment of his Designs, and Fears of something to ensue by this Discovery far worse: And the other, in Tenderness abus'd, and the Reflection on the irreparable Ruin her Inadvertancy had brought upon her, the most poynant Remorse was now the Portion of her Soul; and Dread, and the sharpest Stings of Guilt and Horror his.

The Condition of the perfidious *Clitander* was so much the more perplex'd than that of *Althea*, by the Addition of Uncertainty in what Manner he should proceed; while that unhappy Lady, in the Midst of her Griefs found some little Ease in Resolution, and determin'd to quit a House which had been so fatal to her Virtue and her Peace; and justly detesting the Sight of her Undoer, as soon as she was inform'd *Miranda* was stirring, she sent to desire she would come into her Chamber, who immediately complying with her Request, she told her, That finding herself of late very much indispos'd she believ'd it owing to the Town Air, which by Reason she was not accustom'd to live in, did not agree with her Constitution, and that she would return to her Country Seat, at least, till she had recover'd her former Health. Her present Condition having render'd her Looks more pale and wan than ordinary, contributed to make this Excuse pass current; and her Sister, tho' extreamly concern'd to loose the Pleasure of her Company, thought it would seem rather an Argument of Self-love than the contrary, to press her Stay.

While the two Sisters were engag'd in this Conversation, *Clitander*, who was alone in the Dining-room, was in all the Agonies which Guilt or Fear can inflict; he had heard *Althea*'s Servant desire his Wife to come to her Mistress, and he knew not but the Violence of that Rage with which she was animated against him, might oblige her to relate the whole Story of their Intreague to her Sister. He was sensible, that

Passion of what Kind soever, has small Regard to Prudence; especially in a Female Mind, and began to accuse himself of Weakness, that he had not put an End to his Apprehensions, by depriving her of the Power of Complaining,—with how much Ease, said he to himself, might I have strangled or smother'd the fond Reproacher, as soon as I perceiv'd she took upon her to pry into my Meanings,—I might have left her breathless, to be found by the first comer into the Room,—the Act wou'd have appear'd her own,—No-body wou'd have suspected me,—perhaps my Wife might have made the first Discovery, and the Shock of such a Sight might have been fatal too to her, and I had been rid of both at once,—Fool that I was, and too, too careless of my own Safety, Interest, or Reputation,—shou'd her wild Rage disclose the fatal Secret, I am undone in all without Redemption, lost to all the Views of my aspiring Soul, nay pointed at, and hiss'd as I pass by the demure inhabitants of this well-order'd City. In this Manner did he torment himself, till seeing the Servants run busily up and down the House, he call'd to know the Meaning of this unusual Hurry, and was by one of them inform'd, that *Althea* being going out of Town, they were employ'd in packing up her Things, and preparing for her Departure. If he was before alarm'd, he now was much more so; this sudden Removal made him not doubt but that she had betray'd everything, and unable to endure the just Upbraidings he expected to meet from both these injur'd Ladies, he flew out of the House immediately, resolving not to return till the Absence of one of them might the better encourage him to deny the whole Affair to the other.

He had been but just gone out, when *Miranda* came into the Room where she had left him, to acquaint him with her Sister's Resolution, and missing him, sent everywhere in Search of him, to take Leave of *Althea*: But he was no where to be found, he went a quite contrary Way from any Place where he cou'd be expected, and came not home till very late at Night.

The wretched *Althea* found a kind of gloomy Satisfaction, that she was not oblig'd to dissemble a Civility to the Author of her Ruin, and made what Haste she cou'd away, left any of those sent to seek him shou'd suceed in their Endeavours: But he returning not till Night, was immediately eas'd of his Apprehensions, by the Person that open'd the Door, who acquainted him with the fruitless Search which had been made for him, and the Reason of it. A little more compos'd now in Mind, he had the Power of inventing an Excuse to his Wife for his running away in so abrupt a Manner, which she, wholly free from any Suspicion of the Truth, readily believ'd.

The villanously bent *Clitander* cou'd not, however, be satisfy'd while there remain'd even a Possibility of his Crime being made known; he resolv'd therefore, by some Means or other to put an End to *Althea*, whose Life he look'd on as a continual Danger; but as there was no Opportunity to compass this Design while they were at Variance, he endeavour'd by his former Artifices to gain a Reconciliation. She had not left his House three Days, before he sent her the following Letter.

To the most Lovely, but too Rigorous *Althea*

By this, I hope, Passion has had Time to cool, and Reason has got the Better of unjust Resentment,—Oh! cou'd I ere have thought *Althea*, who seem'd all heavenly Softness, wou'd have so far been deasned by her mistaken Rage, as not to hear *Clitander,* her once lov'd *Clitander* plead!—I confess indeed, that I deceiv'd you as to the *Title* of the Instrument you had order'd me to get drawn up, but the *Design* was still the fame; and it appear'd to me, and to the Lawyer, whose Advice I took, to be more firm and valid this Way than that other we had agreed on: The Motives which induc'd me to it are too long to be inserted here, but if you will permit a Visit from me, I can easily convince you that what I did was wholly owing to my Care to that dear Babe, which next to its charming Mother, must be most precious to my Soul.—Oh! my forever lov'd,—forever ador'd *Althea*, tho' I doubt not but I shall hear you own you have been to blame, and with your usual Softness avow *Clitander*'s Truth, yet the Remembrance that I have been once suspected by you, will be an eternal Vulture to my aking Heart.—Confidence, as it is the greatest *Proof* of a perfect Passion, so it is also the highest *Blessing* of it; Resume it then thou dear, unjust Disturber of thy own Repose, and know *Clitander* better than to admit one Thought to the Prejudice of his Love or Honour; the inchanting Charms which dwell upon thy Mind and Person render it impossible for me to falsify the one, and the Principles in which my Youth was bred wou'd make me chuse Death rather than be guilty of sinning against the other;—how much then haft thou injur'd me, *Althea!*—what Torments has thy unkind Distrust inflicted on me! —My Soul, which flatter'd itself with the Belief it held so perfect an Intelligence with thine, that whatsoever pass'd in one Breast was to the other known, now starts with wild Amaze, and all its Faculties seem lost in Grief and Wonder.—O haste to cure the Wounds thy Cruelty has caus'd, and let the Balsom of returning Love restore once more *Clitander* to himself,—for I am nothing, while depriv'd of thee, but a poor walking Statue, discover'd but by Dispair to have any Remains of Sense or Reason left.— Write to me some Lines of Comfort, and consent to receive once more into thy Esteem, into thy Sight, into thy Arms, the most ardent and sincerest Lover that ever own'd the Power of Beauty;—be doubly kind to make me Reparation for the Wrong thou hast done me, and know that it is the fix'd Determination of my Mind to dye if you persist in this Injustice, it being better not be at all, than not to be

The Divine *Althea's*

Clitander

Whoever has been acquainted with the Force of Love, need not be told what kind of Emotions those are, which of Consequence swell the Bosom of a Person in the Circumstances *Althea* was; never had Woman been possest of a more violent Passion than she was for *Clitander*, nor cou'd any Heart be capable of a greater Resentment than was hers, since the Discovery of his Deceit; she cou'd not read those tender Expressions he had made use of in his Letter, without a Flood of forgiving Softness pouring in upon her Soul; nor cou'd she reflect afterwards that 'twas possible they might be only owing to that Artifice, with which he had attempted to impose on her Credulity, without an Addition to the Rage she was before inspir'd with.—At sometimes she was inclin'd to hear what he cou'd alledge in his Vindication, at others, not to admit of any Excuse; and what she endur'd in the Conflict, between Tenderness and Indignation, is not to be describ'd; the former, however, got at length the Victory; and the same fatal Softness which had at first betray'd her, now sway'd her Inclinations to a second yielding, and all the Remains of Severity she had left was, not to let him immediately be sensible of his Power and her own Weakness and Irresolution. If not so guilty as I at first believ'd, said she to herself, he yet has been to blame in endeavouring to deceive a Heart he might have persuaded.—He shall not, therefore, know my Easiness to pardon,—I will write to him with the same Rigour with which I spoke when last we parted: Nor can I err in this, if he be in Reality the true, the faithful Lover he pretends, his Constancy will abide this little Trial; and if, (as 'tis too possible, that he who cou'd be false in one Thing may in others also) the seeming Softness of these Lines shou'd all be Counterfeit, and a second Imposition, I shall at least prevent him of the Triumph he expects. Thus did this unhappy Victim of an ungovernable Passion, argue with herself, and fancy'd no-body cou'd arrive at a greater Height of Heroism than she was Mistress of, in so far restraining the Dictates of her Tenderness, as to be able to answer him in these Terms.

To the Thankless and Ungenerous *Clitander*

If anything cou'd have added to the Astonishment which the Discovery of your Perfidiousness created, it wou'd be to find you still entertain an Opinion of me so contrary to what I am, or ought to be.—No, no Clitander; it is not in the Power of all your Artifices to deceive me twice;—to know you have been false in one Thing, convinces me there is a Possibility you may be so in all; and, as you too justly for your own Interest observe, Confidence alone makes Love a Blessing; as your Behaviour, therefore, has taken from me the one, I must endeavour to expel the other also, or be forever wretched.—Am I not undone—rnin'd beyond Redemption—by my unhappy Passion reduc'd to a Condition in which Life, Honour, Reputation, everything that is dear must be expos'd to Dangers, infinite and numberless; yet in this dreadful Hazard of my Soul what had I to comfort me but thy believ'd Integrity, and that thou hast destroy'd; and I am now all Misery and Despair, without one chearing Hope, one Dawn of Consolation.—Oh why Clitander wou'd you abuse a Faith so entirely dependant as was mine?—If there were Reasons for altering the intended Will into a Deed of Gift, why was I not acquainted with them?—Heavens! when I reflect with what a zealous Haste you press'd my tardy Hand to sign that Writing, and with what a ready Cunning you turn'd the Words so much the Reverse of what they were, it makes you seem, to my distracted Thought, a Man long practis'd in Deceit, vers'd in Hypocrisy, and kill'd in every Wile of your betraying Sex.—Oh what a dismal Change is this from that dear Character which won me first to Tenderness, and made me think all Things a Virtue which thy Love requir'd.—But to what End does my afflicted Soul thus pour forth her Complainings, if thou art false, thou wilt but scorn my Griefs; if true, they are unjust;—Oh that they were, and that indeed, I cou'd in the Assurance they were so, confess I did amiss, and once more subscribe myself

The too lovely Clitander's
Althea

Having concluded this Epistle, she read it over, and thinking some Part of it express'd too great a Tenderness, to prevent him from entertaining any Hopes, which might be too presuming, she added a Postscript which contain'd these Words:

I wou'd not have you imagine, that because my Heart still avows some Softness at the Remembrance of our former Loves, that it can so much overpower my Reason as to sway me to any Thoughts of a Reconciliation, at least, as yet,—Time, and your future Behaviour can only decide what 'tis I ought to do.—Make no Endeavours therefore for an Interview, left you should alarm a Resentment, which you deceive yourself when you believe is lull'd asleep.

Farewell

Clitander had too often experienc'd the Irresolution of a Female Mind when agitated by that undoing Passion, not to fee *Althea* was as much his own as ever, and that there wanted but a few Oaths and tender Pressures to compleat what his Letter had begun: But as all the Ardours of Desire were now extinguish'd in him, and he no longer aim'd at the Enjoyment of her, he wou'd not seem too forward in his Hopes; his Design being only to keep her Mind in Play, till he shou'd get an Opportunity to rid himself at once of all his Fears, by making her away. Continuing therefore to counterfeit the despairing Lover, soon after the Receipt of hers he sent a second Billet, the Contents whereof were as follows.

To the Dear, Unkind *Althea*

If you had ever any Reason for Surprize in the Behaviour of *Clitander*, it is only now to find he is yet alive after so terrible a Testimony of your Indifference, as that your Letter gave me.—Yes, thou relentless, thou tyrannick Charmer, I yet survive the Loss of Love, but in a Condition, such as were there not a Power whose Indignation is more than even *Althea*'s to be dreaded, wou'd make me gladly fly to Death for Ease.—Were I, indeed, the false, the perjur'd Wretch you think me, how little Effect wou'd your Displeasure have!—Nay, how satisfy'd wou'd some inconsistent Lovers be of such a Pretence to part!—but, Oh *Althea!* I am not of that Number, my Heart wholly made up of Truth and Tenderness, disavows the Maxims of my Sex, and doats upon thee, thou Soul of Pleasure, with the same unabated Fondness, as when I first receiv'd the glorious Recompence of my Pains, and triumph'd in Possession of thy Beauties.—How often have I thought our Minds were pair'd by Heaven, and that we two were chose from the unnumber'd Millions of Mankind, to prove the Immortality of a perfect Passion. No Woman sure, but my *Althea*, cou'd e'er inspire such Raptures; no Man but her *Clitander* cou'd be so sensible of her Power of charming.—Oh think upon the blissful Moments of our Love!—bring back in Idea our past Endearments! remember to what a vast Excess of unrestrain'd Delight we have been transported; and while the extatick Image is in View, judge of the Fervour of *Clitander*'s Flame.—Didst thou deceive me with pretended Softness, and play the Hypocrite in Pleasure? O no, thy Raptures were substantial and sincere; nor cou'd the Soul, when thus disolv'd in Joy, find Room for feigning.—Were mine so enervate, that thou canst doubt their Truth?—thou dear, unjust Disturber! to thy own Heart let me appeal, by that I will be acquitted or condemn'd.—Grant a speedy Answer to my Prayers, but consider, that on what you write depends the Fate of

Your Impatient Slave
Clitander

What now became of *Althea*'s Resolution! her Soul, unus'd to Artifice, no longer cou'd restrain its struggling Tenderness, each thrilling Vein confest rekindled Passion, and the soft Fire diffus'd itself through every glowing Fibre:—No more had she the Power to conceal Desire, no more cou'd listen to the Dictates of Reason or Refentment, and again melted by those destructive Languishments which had at first betray'd her Virtue; she suffer'd her Pen to convince him of a Truth, which before he had little Cause to doubt, and wholly forgetful of all Considerations but those her Love inspir'd, answer'd him in this Manner.

To the too Charming *Clitander*

By what magick Spells, thou dear Enchanter, dost thou work upon my Soul! how in a Moment is it in thy Power to reverse my most fix'd Resolves, now form my Mind, and as thou pleasest tune every jarring Thought! in spite of all I had determin'd, in spite of the Suggestions of my Reason, which tell me, this second Folly is more shameful, even than the former, I confess the Prevalence of thy too fatal Charms, and once more own myself all thine.—O why Clitander! *dost thou alarm Reflection with the Remembrance of those ruinous Delights which I had sworn to taste no more; am I not already too guilty without adding Perjury to the Number of my Offences?—will not all the Pleas of Love, and Nature, appear too weak to excuse my Crimes, and bribe the justice of that dread Tribunal, to which, perhaps, I shortly shall be summon'd?—O! exert thy utmost Wit and Eloquence to arm me against this Thought, and reconcile the two great Opposites,* Desire *and* Virtue,—*with healing Arguments, if possible, case my Despair, and keep me, while on Earth, from sharing the Torments the Damn'd endure. But first, for O! there is no Hell like that of thy Perfidiousness, convince me that my Fears were groundless, and that there was, indeed, no other Motive but our common Interest for that Alteration in the intended Legacy, the sooner I hear your Reasons, the sooner my Inquietudes will cease; but be sure to come prepar'd with such as shall entirely banish all Distrust of their Validity; and give me no Pretence to be any other than what I wish myself,*

My Dear, Ador'd Clitander's
Althea

If *Clitander's* Entreaty for a Reconciliation had sprung from a Desire of re-enjoying her, he had now sufficient to fit him for the utmost Transports; but alas! the Pleasure her Condescension yielded, was of a far different Kind from that which Love inspires: Her Death, which he now found was the only Means both to ease him of all his Fears of Discovery, and to give him the Possession of her Estate, was what he wanted; and the Opportunity her recover'd Kindness promis'd him of executing that horrid Purpose, spread a sullen Satisfaction over all his Soul: The Means he had projected to bring it about was in this Manner:

He had for a great while had an Intimacy with a neighbouring Apothecary, which he improv'd during the Time of his holding this distant Correspondence with *Althea*, but still preserving his old Maxim of depending only on himself, wou'd not let him into any Part of his Designs, but taking all Occasions of running into his Shop, and talking with him in a free Manner, wou'd sometimes ask him what was in one Drawer, and sometimes what was in another; which Intelligence, join'd with his own Understanding in the *Latin* Tongue, made him perfectly acquainted with the Name and Nature of most of those Drugs which furnish out one of those Shops. Amongst the Number there was one, on which he kept a constant Eye; his Friend had told him, that it was a Poison of that deadly Quality, that without the Person who should take it, had very well prepar'd his Body by extraordinary Antidotes, all the Art in the World had not the Power to expel. This was a Dose proper for the Design of this remorseless Wretch, and he resolv'd to play the Thief for some Portion of it, the first Moment Fortune should present him with an Opportunity: According to his Desires he soon met one, the Apothecary happening to be abroad one Day when he came there, and no Person in the Shop but a young A prentice, whom he sent out on some Pretence, he ran immediately to the Drawer, and taking out a sufficient Quantity of that fatal Drug, put it into a Piece of Paper, and conceal'd it in his Pocket-book.

Being thus in Possession of the Treasure he so much coveted, he wanted nothing but the Means of applying it, which also he obtain'd in a short Time: The Anniversary of *Miranda's* Birth-day happening a Day or two after that, in which he had receiv'd that tender Letter from her Sister, he thought he cou'd not chuse a fitter Season for the Accomplishment of his cruel Aim: With a well counterfeited Tenderness, he therefore told that unsuspecting Wife, that he would keep that Day with a Solemnity proportionable to the Tenderness he had for her, and accordingly sent

Invitations to all the Friends on both Sides, to come to his House and partake of an Entertainment he order'd to be provided in Honour of the Day: And at the same Time wrote a private Billet to *Althea*, conjuring her not to fail being there, telling her that if she attempted to evade it by any Excuse, it might create some Suspicion among the Relations, that there was not so good an Agreement between them as usual; and as there was a Time approaching, in which she wou'd be oblig'd to abscond, it wou'd be best for her to appear as long as her Condition would permit; especially at a Time, when her Absence wou'd be look'd on as a Thing so particular, that everyone wou'd be apt to enquire into the Cause. But he needed not have given himself the Trouble of urging so many Arguments, the Desire she had of seeing him again, was a sufficient Inducement of her coming, and now not doubting, because he had told her so, but that at their next private Meeting he wou'd be able to clear himself of everything she cou'd lay to his Charge, was easily persuaded to admit the Reconciliation, before she receiv'd the Reasons for it. In fine, the Day being arriv'd, *Clitander* had the Pleasure of seeing his intended Prey readily fall into the Snare prepar'd for her; and the Success of his Designs made his Eyes sparkle with a Delight, which the deceiv'd *Althea* observing, imagin'd was owing to his Love and Tenderness. There was too much Company to give them any Opportunity for Conversation, but such as was general; but what was deny'd to their Tongues, their speaking Looks seem'd abundantly to make up for.—Unutterable Joy appear'd to revel amidst the soft Beseechings of his Glances, while her's stream'd with ten thousand nameless Languishments, the Badges of Desire, and Simptoms of a Soul dissolv'd.

After a magnificent Collation they went to Country-dancing, where this perfidious Wretch having *Althea* for his Partner, resolv'd no longer to delay the Execution of his abhorr'd Intent, and taking the Opportunity of being the lower Couple, step'd to the *Beaufett*, and filling out a Glass of Wine, drank to her, with these Words: May this blest Moment, said he, put an End to all distrust between us, and be the Beginning of an everlasting Peace to both. With how much Joy I pledge that Health, Thou who knowest my Soul, be Judge, reply'd she; at the same Time looking on him with Eyes so sweetly languishing, that any Heart but his wou'd have relented and melted with Tenderness and Penitence: Yet was he all obdurate and unshock'd, no Starts, no Tremblings confess'd the guilty Secret, no Change of Countenance betray'd the horrid Purpose he was about to act, but keeping the cursed Drug conceal'd between his Thumb and Finger, as he was pouring out the Wine, dropt it into the Glass, unperceiv'd, unsuspected by the unhappy *Althea*, who took it from his remorseless Hand, and drank it to the Bottom.

They continued dancing a considerable Time, nor had the Company any Design of breaking up, when *Althea* finding herself extreamly disorder'd, surpriz'd them with taking a hasty Leave. *Miranda* perceiving she was indispos'd, wou'd have persuaded her to lye there, or to suffer some of her People to wait on her home; but she refus'd both, imagining that her Illness proceeded only from her being lac'd more strait that Day than ordinary, to conceal the Alteration in her Shape, from giving any Suspicion of the Condition which had occasion'd it. Nobody looking on her Distemper as dangerous, they suffer'd her to depart, without giving any Interruption to the Gaiety, which *Clitander* took Care nothing shou'd be wanting to inspire among them.

But this abus'd Lady had not gone many Streets, before she found her Pains encrease in so terrible a Manner, that she was unable to sustain them, without endeavouring some Relief.—She knew there were many Months between that, and the Time in which she must expect those Agonies which all, in becoming Mothers, feel; and incapable of ascribing any Cause for what she endur'd, call'd out to the Coachman to stop at the House of an Apothecary, who on all Occasions was us'd to attend their Family, and liv'd in the Way she was to pass. Happening to find him at home, she suffer'd herself to be led into a Parlour, where she was no sooner set down, but she found herself grow worse; and in a few Moments swell'd to that prodigious Degree, that her Laceings burst, her Eyes seem'd to start out of her Head, and every Feature was distorted. The skilful Apothecary immediately cry'd out that she was poison'd, and ran to fetch Things proper to expel it, but the Malignity had spread itself too far, and all that he cou'd do was ineffectual: Fearing, however, to depend on his own Art, he sent for an Eminent Physician to come there, she now being in a Condition which would not admit of her being remov'd: But on the first Sight of her, he made no Scruple of revealing the sad Truth, That it was not in the Power of Art to save her. Is it then certain, said she, that I must dye? Nothing less than a Miracle can preserve you, Madam, answer'd he. These Words pronounc'd with a grave and assur'd Accent, join'd to the intollerable Pains which every Moment encreas'd upon her, made her not doubt, but that her Condition was desperate indeed; and in the Extremity of her Anguish, forgetful of all other Considerations but those which the Horrour of her Fate inspir'd, she cry'd aloud, that all in the House were Witnesses of the Exclamations, Then I am poison'd by *Clitander*, that murderous Villain has kill'd both the Life and Honour of the lost *Althea*:—Oh! I am doubly damn'd, first by the Crime he drew me to commit, and next by my Knowledge to what a Monster I have sacrific'd my Virtue.— Such Expressions seem'd to have a Meaning in 'em too dreadful not to make those who heard them press her to explain herself more fully; both the Doctor and Apothecary entreated she would give them the Particulars of what she seem'd to intimate, but cou'd get nothing from her but the same Words several Times repeated; perceiving that either her bodily Torments, or those of her Mind, had driven her into a kind of Despair, they ask'd her if she was not willing to consult a Spiritual Physician: To which she reply'd, That she was past all Hope of Relief, either in this World, or that to which the was going; and immediately fell into Rayings so horrible and shocking, that they imprinted a Terror on the Minds of those present, which for a great while they were not able to wear off. Never did the Idea of Futurity appear so dreadful, as that which her Behaviour inspir'd nor never came Death accompany'd with Tormenis such as hers.—The most guilty Wretch that suffers the Sentence of the Law has, with the Certainty of his Fate, a Time for Preparation for it allow'd him, but she had none, taken in the very Fulness of her Crimes; and by those racking Pains which every convuls'd Nerve, and starting Vein sustain'd, render'd incapable of Penitence, of Prayer, or Consolation. A Minister of that Religion she profest bang sent for, he exhorted her by all the Admonitions he was capable of making, to endeavour to compole her Mind, and throw herself on the Mercy of all-gracious Heaven, but the wou'd not suffer him to speak on that Head.—Talk not of Mercy, said she, I have finn'd beyond the Reach of Pardon,—I am already damn'd, wou'd she sometimes roar out, —a Thousand Fiends encompass me about,—they wait to seize my Soul;—and then again, more wildly, Now, now I burn, cry'd she, now feel the Flames which are decreed for Adultery and Incest. In this Manner did she continue all that Night, and early in the Morning the Apothecary thinking it proper not to conceal the Condition she was in, sent a Person whom he cou'd consider in, to the House of *Clitander*, to acquaint *Miranda* with the fatal News.

That Lady being yet in Bed, the Messenger, who said he must needs speak to her that Moment, was order'd to come into her Chamber, where having told her in what Manner he left her Sister, and related some Part of those Expressions her Despair had made her utter, reduc'd her to a Condition almost as pityable, she sainted away several Times while she was preparing to make herself ready to go; and indeed it is rather to be wonder'd at, that in so dreadful a Juncture, and in so unconceivably terrible a Surprize, that she retain'd Strength enough of Mind be bear the Sight of what she heard, than that she endur'd so much in the attempting it. She arriv'd not however at the Scene of Misery till her unhappy Sister was no more: The Moment of her Entrance, was that in which the afflicted Soul forsook its wretched Mansion, leaving that once lovely and Desirecreating Form, the most terrible and ghastly Spectacle, that ever made the View of Death a Horror. *Miranda* was for sometime incapable either of making any Demands, or listening to any Informations, but as soon as she was in a Condition, receiv'd from the Mouths of the Divine, the Doctor, the Apothecary, and all his Family, a Confirmation of what the Messenger had said. The Reader's Imagination must here assist my Pen, or it will be impossible for him to form any just Notion of what the endur'd in the killing Repetition of so dreadful an Account. I shall only say, that she sustain'd it with Life, and that was all. It was the Opinion of everybody that *Althea* shou'd be open'd, to which, it being propos'd to *Miranda*, she consented, nor wou'd leave the House till it was done, still hoping that the Surgeons who perform'd that Operation, might find someother Cause than Poison for her Death: But alas! how terrible a Surcharge to her Afflictions did the receive, when they acquainted her that That fair Unfortunate not only receiv'd her Death by those Means the Doctor and Apothecary had said, but also, that she was with Child; and to prove the Truth of what they told her, presented her with an Embrio of at least six Months Growth. This wretched, yet still tender Wife had now no Comfort left, but in the distant Possibility that her Husband might be wrong'd, and that in Spite of what the Deceas'd had declar'd, someother Man might have been the Father of the Child, and Author of this double Murder; but soon this Shadow of a Consolation fled, and she became all Misery and Despair: Remembring that when she first came into the Room, she saw a Pocket-Book of her Sister's lying on the Ground, she desir'd it might be search'd for, imagining that there might be something which wou'd give her a further Discovery of what she with'd, yet dreaded to be assur'd. Accordingly it did, for it being immediately produc'd, she found, to the inexpressible Shock of all those Hopes with which the endeavour'd to flatter herself, those two Letters before incerted here, and that last fatal one which drew her wretched Sister to her Deftiny.—Which, to satisfy the Curiosity of my Reader, and more to expose the monstruous Villany of the impious *Clitander*, I will also give a Copy of.

To the Most Excellent *Althea*

With what Words, O thou Perfection on of all Loveliness! shall I make you sensible of the Ecstacies that fill'd my ravish'd Soul, at the forgiving Goodness of your last charming Letter;—sure I am, no Language can reach the vast Extent of Love and Joy like mine!—The unequall'd Softness of thy own endearing Thoughts can best inform thee what thy *Clitander* feels in this Restoration of his long languishing, and almost expiring Hopes!—Desire, sunk to Despair, revives and gladens with redoubled Ardour!—O how I long to read in those dear Eyes the blest Confirmation of what thy Pen declares,—Soon wou'd I fly to seize the Transport, but that the Birth-day of *Miranda* being so near, I take that Opportunity, under the Pretence of Tenderness, to celebrate my Reconciliation with *Althea*.—O may that Day put a Period to all future Misunderstandings between us, and compleat *Clitander*'s Happiness.—I beg you, by all the Tenderness you have profest, and which still sways your gentle Soul, to commiserate my Pains, not to fail blessing me with your Presence on that Day: You know, my Angel, that a Time will shortly arrive in which you must be oblig'd to shun the Converse of your Friends, and it will be of Service to your Reputation, as well as to my eager Wishes, for you to appear as long as possible: Shou'd you be absent, not only your own distant Relations, but also *Miranda* herself wou'd be surpriz'd; and who knows on what Enquiries it might put some People? But that Motive, which I flatter myself will most induce you to comply is, that it is entreated by him, who I hope you soon will cease to doubt if he is

The most adorable *Althea*'s
Truest and Everlasting Slave
Clitander

To know what kind of Emotions those were which swell'd the Breast of this distress'd Lady, at reading these Letters, which the too well knew were written by her Husband's Hand, one must be in the Circumstances she was; but it is notwithstanding very easy to guess her Agonies were the most terrible that Humanity cou'd support. She had lov'd him with too sincere a Tenderness for even this plain Detection of his Villany presently to obliterate, she cou'd not resolve to prosecute him in that Manner which his Crime deserv'd, yet was not so blinded by her Passion, as to forget what she ow'd to the Memory of her injur'd Sister, the Wrong he had done herself, and indeed the just Care of her own future Safety, as to think of living with a Monster, who she now found would scruple nothing. Making therefore very few Replies to the Invectives the heard utter'd against him, nor speaking anything of the Discovery which the Letters had made, she took her Leave of the Appothecary, telling him that he should hear further from her, and withdrew to the House of a Relation, who had formerly been her Guardian; whence the sent by a Porter the following Billet to her perfidious Husband.

I Need not tell you that my Sister is no more, you know
but too well that she cou'd not live, and doubtless are by
this Time inform'd that I was sent for, to see the Last of
that unhappy Wretch.—I believe you will scarce expect
my Return to a Place, where I must every Duy behold a
Villain, who not content with murdering her Honour, took
away also her Life, with that of the innocent Product of his
incestuous Passion,—I wish to Heaven the dreadful Secret
were only known to me, but in the Agonies of her departing
Soul herself declar'd it to too many, for you, I fear, to escape
the Punishment your Guilt deserves:—Take Care, therefore,
of yourself, for you will stand in need of all your Wit and
Artifice to shield you from the Sword of Justice.—This
Caution is the last Proof of Kindness you will ever receive
from

Your Greatly Injur'd and
Unfortunate Wife
Miranda

Early as it was in the Morning, when the Person sent by the Apothecary came to *Miranda, Clitander* uneasy till he knew the

Consequence of last Night's Action, had forsook his Beed, and was gone to give a Loose to Thought in a retir'd Walk, which he very much frequented, but not being able to rest there, he went from Coffee-House to Coffee-House, endeavouring but in Vain, some Ceffation of his perplex'd Imaginations; at length returning home, was told in what Manner *Miranda* had been call'd out, and the Condition she was in at some News brought her by the Person who came to her: This fill'd him with mortal Disquiets, which the Receipt of the forgoing Letter confirm'd. He had hop'd the Poison wou'd have taken Effect, and destroy'd her in a more sudden Manner, and began now to be apprehensive, that all the Secrecy he had made use of wou'd stand him but in little Stead.—As for his Wife's Resentment, it gave him but little Pain, since he perceiv'd she wou'd not appear as an Evidence against him; he thought it best however to take the Advice she gave him, and withdraw, till he should hear if anything was design'd against him or not, and accordingly went out of Town that very Night, entrusting no one with the Place of his Retirement, but a near Relation, to whom he also committed the Care of his House, and who sent him from Time to Time an Account of everything, and receiv'd his Instructions how to proceed.

Miranda declining the Prosecution of her Husband, those to whom *Althea* had declar'd the fatal Mistery of his Guilt, were the only Persons whom *Clitander* had Reason to fear; and on being inform'd that they talked pretty freely of the Affair, and mingled some Menaces with their Discourse of it, gave Orders to his Friend to act in this Manner: He went to each of them, and acquainting them with the Knowledge he had of their Suspicions, and the Reasons they had for it, told them they ought not to judge by Appearances; that in Case *Clitander* were guilty, there was no Possibility of proving him so, the Lady who had accus'd him having been Lunatick for sometime before her Death, and besides it was wholly inconsistant with Reason to believe him both her Lover and her Poisoner; it seem'd more probable, that being with Child, to conceal her Shame she had taken something to destroy it, which had work'd an Effect contrary to what she design'd, than that it should be given her by any other Person: And concluded these Arguments with a Remonstrance, that to go about to prosecute a Man for a Crime, of which at most he cou'd but be suppos'd guilty, wou'd only involve the Persons who did it, in a great deal of Trouble, and be of no Service either to restore the Life, or revenge the Death of the Person for whole Sake they undertook it. These Considerations, by Degrees made an

Impression in the Minds of those to whom they were address'd, which, together with everyone having Business which was more his own, join'd to make, the Ghost of this wrong'd Lady remain yet unappeas'd, and the wicked *Clitander* triumph in the Belief, That neither Heaven not Earth will take any further Notice of his Crimes.

For the Sake of his Reputation, however, he made use of all his Cunning to be reconcil'd to his Wife; and might, perhaps, have impos'd on her Belief as much as on that of others, had not the Letters found in the dead *Althea*'s Pocket-Book, been an undeniable Witness of his Guilt.—She keeps them by her, and daily reads them over, to preserve in Memory his Offences, and prevent his Artifices from the Success he aims at. The Knowledge how much he is in the Power of one he has to highly injur'd, is a perpetual Rack upon his Spirits, and in infinitely more reasonable Apprehensions of Danger on her Account, than ever he had on that of *Althea*; While *here*, he suffers a Taste of that Bitterness of Soul; which in greater Abundance he must *hereafter* swallow to all Eternity; having reap'd no other Advantage from all the monstruous Villanies he acted, than an Augmentation of those Disquiets which an unsatiated Avarice creates.

FINIS

A Note About the Author

Eliza Haywood (1693–1756) was an English novelist, poet, playwright, actress, and publisher. Notoriously private, Haywood is a major figure in English literature about whom little is known for certain. Scholars believe she was born Eliza Fowler in Shropshire or London, but are unclear on the socioeconomic status of her family. She first appears in the public record in 1715, when she performed in an adaptation of Shakespeare's *Timon of Athens* in Dublin. Famously portrayed as a woman of ill-repute in Alexander Pope's *Dunciad* (1743), it is believed that Haywood had been deserted by her husband to raise their children alone. Pope's account is likely to have come from poet Richard Savage, with whom Haywood was friends for several years beginning in 1719 before their falling out. This period coincided with the publication of *Love in Excess* (1719–1720), Haywood's first and best-known novel. Alongside Delarivier Manley and Aphra Behn, Haywood was considered one of the leading romance writers of her time. Haywood's novels, such as *Idalia; or The Unfortunate Mistress* (1723) and *The Distress'd Orphan; or Love in a Madhouse* (1726), often explore the domination and oppression of women by men. *The History of Miss Betsy Thoughtless* (1751), one of Haywood's final novels, is a powerful story of a woman who leaves her abusive husband, experiences independence, and is pressured to marry once more. Highly regarded by feminist scholars today, Haywood was a prolific writer who revolutionized the English novel while raising a family, running a pamphlet shop in Covent Gardens, and pursuing a career as an actress and writer for some of London's most prominent theaters.

A Note from the Publisher

Spanning many genres, from non-fiction essays to literature classics to children's books and lyric poetry, Mint Edition books showcase the master works of our time in a modern new package. The text is freshly typeset, is clean and easy to read, and features a new note about the author in each volume. Many books also include exclusive new introductory material. Every book boasts a striking new cover, which makes it as appropriate for collecting as it is for gift giving. Mint Edition books are only printed when a reader orders them, so natural resources are not wasted. We're proud that our books are never manufactured in excess and exist only in the exact quantity they need to be read and enjoyed.

Discover more of your favorite classics with Bookfinity™.

- Track your reading with custom book lists.
- Get great book recommendations for your personalized Reader Type.
- Add reviews for your favorite books.
- AND MUCH MORE!

Visit **bookfinity.com** and take the fun Reader Type quiz to get started.

Enjoy our classic and modern companion pairings!